Picking Worms

Book One
of
The Campfire Boys

Doreen Millichamp

authorHOUSE®

AuthorHouse™
1663 Liberty Drive, Suite 200
Bloomington, IN 47403
www.authorhouse.com
Phone: 1-800-839-8640

First published by AuthorHouse 9/4/2007

ISBN: 978-1-4343-2646-1 (sc)

Printed in the United States of America
Bloomington, Indiana

This book is printed on acid-free paper.

Dedicated to my sister Neva St. Dennis
who encouraged me to write my stories down.

Chapter I
The Boys Meet

"Are we there yet?" whined six year old Susie for the tenth time since leaving her home in Toronto.

Dale and John, who were sitting with Susie in the back seat of the family van, rolled their eyes skyward and shook their heads.

"We're just turning onto Crow Lake Campgrounds now," exclaimed Mom! "Hold your horses! We'll set up camp right after we register for the summer."

The Waite's blue van stopped at the gate entrance and the owner of the campground, Mr. Schmitt approached, smiling. "Welcome back," he said. "It's nice seeing familiar faces back on the May long weekend. I kept your usual camp site for you."

Mr. Waite paid the fees for the summer and thanked Mr. Schmitt. Soon they were arriving at their favorite camping spot.

Crow Lake Campgrounds was about 200 kilometers northwest of Toronto. With the Waite family arriving at nine p.m. they had just enough sunlight to set up their camper, kitchen tent, and the boy's blue tent (officially named the Blue Nose). After helping their father stack some firewood at a safe distance from their campfire, the boys were exhausted. Dale, ten years and John, eight years, were thankful their nagging little sister Susie was not sleeping in their tent because they needed privacy. Making one pit stop to the outside wooden toilet, they quickly hopped into their sleeping bags and fell sound asleep within a few minutes. Outside, the stars were sparkling in the night sky like jewels. To the north, there was a hint of the northern Auroras in its colorful display of dancing and swirling lights. The lake was calm and the smell of the outdoors was refreshing.

Early next morning the frogs were croaking and robins were singing outside the Blue Nose when the boys woke up. Dale rolled over in his sleeping bag and looked at his watch.

"I can't lie here anymore. It's six o'clock!" Dale whispered. "Do you want to get up now? If we're quiet, we can walk along the beach shore and see what's there."

"Whatever we do," John said with a yawn, "don't wake mom or dad yet. They like sleeping in."

As fast as the two boys could, they got dressed and left the tent. They started to walk to the sandy beach, which was about two hundred feet from their campsite.   Crow Lake's water was so clear that you could see fish swimming. Near the beach there was a four-foot wide stump of an ancient cedar tree that begged to be climbed on. The brothers walked in silence until they were about one hundred feet from the beachfront.

"Race you to the stump," John said.

Off he ran as fast as he could. Dale followed quickly in his footprints. John's hand touched the old tree stump half a second before Dale. Breathless, they both laughed and hoisted themselves up on the stump and looked about. In the distance the call of a loon echoed across the still misty waters of the lake, and a song of a sparrow was singing in a tree behind them.

"I wonder who we will meet at the camp this year?" John asked.

"I hope Lee comes up again." Dale said. "We had lots of fun last summer. His mom sure makes great egg rolls too."

"What are you doing?" asked a small voice behind them.

Turning around, the boys saw Susie, standing there.

"Mom said for me to tell you boys that breakfast will be ready in half an hour," Susie said. "She knew you were up." She crossed her arms and stared at the boys with a defiant grin.

"Okay, Susie Q," said Dale. "Now go away."

"Nope," said Susie shaking her head. "Mom told me to stick with you boys. So I'm stuck."

John ignored his annoying sister. He looked up the forked road to the third campsite, when he saw Lee Chong come out of his parent's metallic red trailer (named the Red Dragon). John excitedly jumped off the tree stump and ran to him. Shaking him by the shoulders, John said, "Boy, is it good to see you again!" Smiling, he hugged his friend.

Lee beamed back. "I was hoping you boys were here too."

Soon Dale and Susie arrived. Lee messed Susie's hair. "High squirt." Lee turned to Dale. The two boys grabbed each other's hands and gave an enthusiastic secret shake.

"Good to see you, Dale." Lee asked. "How have you been?"

"Just great now that you're here," Lee replied

Lee's mother, Mrs. Wong, stepped out of the screen door of the Red Dragon while holding a cup of her favorite green tea. "Nice to see you boys again," she said. "John, tell your mother I will come over later to visit with her." Mrs. Wong walked over to the kitchen tent and started to unpack some boxes.

Turning to Lee, John asked, "Anyone else here we know?"

"I've only seen one other family with a boy our age down by the bass pond," Lee answered. "I haven't had time to go over there yet. Maybe we can go over there after breakfast."

"Breakfast!" John exclaimed. "Come on," he signaled to Susie and Dale. "We can't keep mom waiting or she'll be on the warpath. See you later, Lee." John waved as he turned to walk away.

The trio walked quickly back to their campsite. The aroma of cooked pancakes and maple bacon, their favorite, drifted to their sniffing nostrils. Their mouths began to water with anticipation. While eating breakfast the family talked about their individual plans for the long weekend. John remembered to tell his mother of Lee's mom coming over for a visit. After breakfast, John and Dale ran over to the Red Dragon. Lee was just coming out the door as they approached.

"Hi again," he said. "Let's go over and see the new kid on the block."

John and Dale nodded. Down the dusty dirt road they marched. Talking a mile a minute, John and Dale were trying to tell Lee what they did over the school year, and Lee was trying to do the same.

Lee pointed across the road. See that silver trailer over there? That's where I saw a boy about our age."

The three of them looked at the trailer then each other and said in unison, "The Silver Bullet", and laughed. The boys had previously started given nicknames to their campsites and the Silver Bullet seemed appropriate. Slowly they approached a shiny silver Air Stream trailer. They noticed two dark African adults sitting outside around a fire pit drinking what smelled like coffee. A very tall, slim, ebony skinned boy walked around from behind the trailer. As he saw the boys approaching, his face brightened into a huge smile showing his large white teeth.

"Salamatta. Hello," he said. "Welcome to our campsite. I'm Amharic Leenco."

Amharic pointed to his parents and said, "This is my mom, Hosituu and my dad, Bunna."

"We're originally from Ethiopia, but now we live in your beautiful Kingston town," he said.

The boys shook hands all around and introduced themselves. They pointed to their trailers and told the Leencos their names: Red Dragon, Blue Nose, and now they would call this trailer the Silver Bullet. The Leencos looked at each other. Mr. Leenco said, "We have a lot to learn about your Canadian customs. Do you name everything?"

"No, the campers laughed. We just do it for fun!"

"The Silver Bullet...... I will have to remember that name," Mr. Leenco said to his wife.

Dale looked at Amharic and asked, "Would you like to join us? We're going to walk around the camp and see if there is anybody else to play with." Amharic nodded his head. He looked at his parents and they also nodded their approval.

Walking slowing up the dirt road, the boys discussed what sports they liked best and who was their greatest star or their favorite sports team. Dale told Amharic about how well the fishing was at the bass pond across from his trailer, and the fishing contest that they would have in two weeks. The noise of a large vehicle coming from behind made the boys turn around. A large dark green Winnebago was slowly making its way along the road. They moved to a grassy area to allow it to pass.

"Boy! Did you see how big that RV was?" declared John. "It's almost as big as a house trailer."

"I wonder where it's going to park?" asked Lee.

The boys watched the RV head on down the dusty road, Dale jumped up and exclaimed, "It's going to the big lot beside our camp. It's the only spot left on this road."

Quickly the four boys ran down to John and Dale's campsite. Sitting around the campfire, captivated, they watched how easily the owner backed the RV into position on the campsite. A couple came out of the trailer and pulled out the kitchen and bedroom extensions on one side of the RV. They secured them with poles. Then they pulled out a wheelchair ramp from under the front passenger door. To the left of this door they cranked down the awning.

"Okay Mark, you can come out now," said the mother.

The RV's door opened and slowly down the ramp rolled an electric wheelchair with a very red haired, freckle-faced boy who looked about nine-years old. Dale and John gave each other high fives. Without a word they all stood and walked over to the boy in the wheelchair. Dale took the initiative and introduced himself and the other boys. Mark was a bit overwhelmed and nervous at first. He looked at the boys and took a big breath.

"My name is Mark MacDougall," he said, "and my wheelchair will take me almost anywhere I want to go."

The boys in turn each walked around and admired Mark's motorized wheelchair. Lee asked, "Hey guys, let's get together after lunch. Can you come Mark?"

Mark's mother overheard their conversation from the other side of the picnic table. As Mark turned to look at her, she said, "Sure you can go Mark. It's nice to meet new friends, but don't go too far."

The boys spent some time getting to know each other that day. They walked and rolled over the entire campgrounds checking out things that they could do during the summer. In the afternoon the boys swam for a short while at the beach because the water was a bit chilling for opening season. They ended up splashing around and making sand castles. Mark watched from his wheelchair and laughed at their antics.

As they were about to go back to their campsites for supper, Mark asked, "How about tomorrow morning at nine we all meet at my place? We can plan our day's adventure then." The newly formed friends agreed.

That evening the Waite family sat laughing and talking around their campfire roasting marshmallows.

About 30 feet away Mark watched for a few minutes from his kitchen tent. He could see the Waite's campfire sending sparks slowly drifting upwards. He could somewhat hear Susie's laughter as some funny story was told. Turning his attention to his parents, who were sitting at the outside tent kitchen table, he said, "I had a great time today. It's good to make new friends." His parents looked at each other and smiled.

Chapter II
Fishing

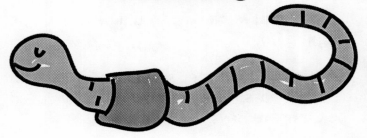

The sun was shining and there were only a few clouds in the sky when the boys met after breakfast at Mark's place, now dubbed the Green Hornet.

"Hey guys, I think we as a group should have a name too," said Dale. He looked around at the others, and then said, "Any ideas?"

"What about The Band of Five?" asked John.

The other boys shook their heads and thought some more.

"I know," said Mark, "We could be called The Campfire Boys."

"Hey, that's a good one," said Lee nodding with the other boys. "We are now officially called The Campfire Boys."

The five boys put their right hands on top of one another, than they threw their hands into the air shouting, "The Campfire Boys!"

After talking for a short while Amharic burst out, "Let's go shore fishing by my place.

"Okay," they yelled back in unison.

"I'll meet you there in a few minutes," shouted Amharic as he walked to his campsite.

Lee ran to the Red Dragon and retrieved his fishing box and rod from under the trailer.

He told his mom where he would be and quickly ran down the dusty road before she could say a word.

Dale and John walked beside Mark as he rolled down the dirt road to the pond.

The pond was the size of two tennis courts and almost perfectly round. It was as deep and clear as a swimming pool. In the middle was lots of dark green water-grass with some lily pads to the south and gravel on the bottom. This pond was the ideal spawning bed for bass fish in the spring. There was a four-foot water entrance that extended about twenty feet from the main lake to the pond. The owner of the campsite would not let anyone swim in it or put in a boat, but he allowed fishing off the shore after spawning. As the boys approached the pond, Amharic who was waiting for them with his fishing gear, waved and walked over to join them. Soon they were spreading out along the sandy water's edge.

Dale said, "I'm using an artificial green frog as bait." He threw his line out as far as he could and reeled it in slowly and repeated this process again and again.

"I like my artificial flavored worm," John replied. He threw his line out on a red and white bobber and waited.

Lee and Amharic used different colored Rapalas. They would cast out and slowly reel in before it reached the bottom of the pond. Mark was able to maneuver his wheelchair within one foot to the edge of the pond. He used a three-foot fishing rod with a live worm on his hook and a yellow and white bobber. Within a few minutes of Mark putting his line out he had a nibble. The fishing line began to giggle, and the bobber bobbed up and down a few times. Mark set the hook by pulling upwards so hard on the fishing rod, that he nearly stood up.

"I've got one!" Mark shouted. "I've got one!"

Amharic's parents across the road looked up as they heard a shout.

Slowly he reeled in his line, but the fish was a fighter. Mark would no sooner reel in a few feet of the fishing line than the fish would fight back with all his might. The irritable fish would struggle and wiggle back and forward. He would pull the fishing line, that he was caught on, as far out to the center of the pond as he could. It was a tug of war between the crabby fish and Mark's determination. Who would win?

The other boys urged Mark on. It took all of his strength to reel the fish up to the shoreline about five minutes later.

Dale reeled in his line and laid his rod down and ran over to Mark. "I'll take the hook out for you," he volunteered. He quickly grabbed the large mouth bass by the gills and with his small red pliers, taken out from his back pocket, Dale gently removed the hook. He held the fish up proudly so all could see.

"My, that's a mighty fine fish you have there," John announced.

Dale placed the prized fish on a fish stringer at the first ringer and put it back in the water to keep it fresh. The stringer was attached to a thin rope tied to a small tree by the pond.

"Now if I can only catch two more for Mom and Dad," Mark said with a smile.

Amharic hadn't seen a fish stringer and was fascinated. Turning to Dale he asked, "How does that stringer work?"

Dale replied, "Each stringer has about six metal loops that open and close. At the end of the stringer is a long rope that we secure to a tree or rock. As we catch fish we put them on the first or second loop, and so on. We put the opened loop through the fish's gill and close the loop. Then we put the fish back in the water to keep it alive. They can swim around, but they cannot get away, as they are attached to the stringer, which is attached to the tree."

"Very interesting," said Amharic nodding his head.

The boys went back to their fishing. About ten minutes later Mark felt the familiar nibbles again and he set the hook like last time, but this time he was more prepared. A moment later Mark hollered with a big huge smile, "I've got another one."

Again he wrestled with the fish for a short time before he could reel it in. It was another large mouth bass. The boys stood around admiring this second fish, which was flopping around on the grass. Dale placed this fish on the second ringer of the stringer and put the wiggling fish back in the water.

Before the boys could go back to their fishing spots, a deep voice from behind them said, "It's the worms that make them bite."

The boys slowly turned around and saw an older man who was slightly bald with grey hair. He had a grey beard parted in the middle of his chin. He had a set of crutches nestling on his arms just below his elbows, and he was wearing a white shirt and blue shorts. Looking downward, they could see that his right leg was amputated from the knee down. The stranger saw that they were looking at his missing leg with their mouths agape.

"Lost it in Vietnam," the stranger said.

Feeling awkward, the boys looked at one another not knowing what to say.

"My name is Hal and I live over there." He pointed to a gold trailer on the lot beside Amharic's. "You need big fat worms," he continued.

"I only have these store bought little worms," replied Mark as he held them out to Hal.

"Well, if you boys get permission to come back here at 9:30 tonight," Hal said, "I'll show you how to catch nice big fat worms. Each of you must bring a small pail with a lid on it, a damp cloth to wipe your hands, and a flashlight." The boys nodded and smiled at each other.

"By the way," Hal added, "for each worm you catch for me, I'll give you a nickel. You can keep how many you want."

Dale looked at John with a grin. "We could make a bundle. It can't be that hard to catch worms."

Lee nodded, "All you have to do is grab those slimy suckers and put them in a pale. Right?"

Amharic agreed saying, " When I was small and back in Ethiopia, we used to dig up some small worms and fry them." With an earnest look he asked the boys, "Do you eat worms here?"

"Ugh, no……..," said John.

The other boys made faces and returned to their fishing spots.

John caught a small perch on his artificial worm. Because the perch was too small, he returned it back to the pond water.

Mark caught one more bass. He returned to his campsite triumphantly and held up his trophy to his parents. His dad cleaned and washed the fish for supper.

Later that day at the Blue Nose campsite, Dale asked his father, "Why didn't the fish bite my artificial frog?"

Mr. Waite answered, "Dale, frogs are usually tempting to bigger fish like pickerel or the big pike that we have in this lake." Poking a stick into the campfire, he continued, "Now worms, that's a different story. They wiggle and jiggle. Almost all fish have a craving for the big fat juicy worms."

"Speaking of worms, dad," Dale said excitedly. "We met a neighbour of Amharic. His name is Hal and he only hast the top part of one of his legs. He's going to show The Campfire Boys how to pick worms tonight. We're sticking all together and coming back together, okay?"

Mr. Waite smiled at his youngest son. "Sounds very interesting. You have my consent boys."

Chapter III
Picking Worms

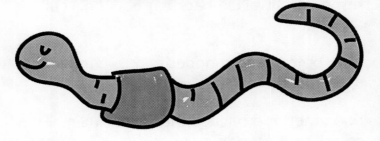

After getting permission and promising to be home by 10:30 that night John, Dale, and Lee walked excitedly along the dirt road to Hal's trailer carrying their required equipment. Mark was rolling along in his electric wheelchair, just ahead of them. The evening sun was slowly sinking over the horizon in the cool May evening. Frogs were croaking from their resting spots on the lily beds, and the fireflies were starting to take to the air, blinking on and off as if to show the boys the way.

"You know, Hal's trailer is gold, and we always give our trailers special names," Dale said as he turned and walked backwards. "Lets call his the Golden Eagle!"

The other boys nodded and mumbled in agreement.

Soon they approached the Silver Bullet. They could see Amharic and his parents sitting around a small campfire. Amharic poked a stick into the fire, sparks rose high into the air and slowly drifted down as they turned to white ash. Looking up, Amharic saw the boys approaching and stood up smiling. The boys waved to Amharic's parents and gestured Amharic to join them as they continued to walk excitedly to Hal's Golden Eagle.

Hearing the boys outside his trailer, Hal limped out on his crutches.

"Are you ready boys?" he asked as he sat on the top trailer step.

Each boy nodded in anticipation. They crowded in close to Hal so they would not miss a single word.

"I want you to listen very carefully to what I say before we begin," said Hal. "The worms like to come out at night with half their body lying on top of the grass and the other half in the ground. They're smart little critters as they can also feel vibrations. So you must be very cautious when you creep up on them. You have to step slowly and quietly." Scratching his gray beard and slowly looking each boy in the eyes, Hal continued.

"One of you can flash the light on them and the other can pick up the worm. Now, it's not that easy to pick up worms. They're slippery critters," he added with a raspy laugh. "You have to grab hold of the first half that is on top of the grass, firmly but not too tight now, or you might break them in half. If they break in half they are no good to you, as they will soon die. You can't put them in the pail with the whole worms because when they die, their decaying bodies can kill the good worms."

Almost whispering, Hal stretched his hand down to the ground and moved his fingers as if they where closing around a worm. "Then, ever so slowly, pull the rest of the worm out of the ground."

"This is where you can start," Hal said, as he pointed to the lush green lawn to the right of his trailer. "I'll sit here and watch."

"I'll stay over here and flash my light so someone can do the picking," said Mark. He wheeled his chair to the side of the road and grass-line and shone his flashlight searching for the worms.

Dale also shone his light around on the grass while the other boys tried to see the worms before walking on the grass.

Hal waved the Leenco family over to enjoy the antics of the boys. They brought their lawn chairs close to his trailer steps and the three of them tried to hide their laughter as the boys crept, tiptoed, and attempted to sneak up on the ever-elusive worms.

John pointed to a nice big fat worm and slowly crept forward on the grass. Just as he bent down, the ever-elusive worm retreated into its little hole. Spotting another, John didn't move his feet, but stretched his arm down and quickly grabbed the worm. The slimy worm wiggled and jiggled until it pulled itself free of John's fingers and slid back into his hole. The same thing was happening to Amharic and Lee. Again and again they tried, but the sneaky worms just kept outsmarting them.

Frustrated, Dale whispered to John: "Here, let me try." John wiped the worm slim off his hands first and then handed him the flashlight.

John shone the light and pointed to another fat worm. Dale took one slow step, reached down and grabbed the worm, determined not to lose it. Pop! The worm broke in half. "Darn! He's as strong as an ox," Dale complained.

For the next frustrating ten minutes the boys tried and tried to catch a worm, but without success.

"It's harder than it looks," said Dale to anybody who was listening.

Barefoot, Amharic zoned in on another nice large juicy worm. He took a quiet step forward to the target. He stretched his long arms down and quickly grabbed the worm. He firmly hung on while the slimy worm struggled to retreat back into its hole. Amharic very slowly pulled back and the worm finally came out of his home wiggling around in his hand. Triumphantly Amharic whooped and put the worm in the pail that Lee was holding. Soon the other boys were starting to get the hang of it too, but they lost more than they caught. A half hour later, Hal called the boys over.

"Okay, I think you're getting the drift of it," he said. "You can try again tomorrow night."

Proudly, looking in their pails, the boys counted ten worms between them.

John walked over to Hal. "Do you still want to buy these worms?" he asked.

Hal nodded his head. "A bargain is a bargain." He reached into his pocket and took out some change. "Here's fifty cents for them. I'm sure you can do better around your own grassy areas tomorrow night."

The boys cheerfully thanked Hal for showing them how to catch the big fat dew worms. After saying goodnight to Amharic and his parents, the rest of the boys returned to their own campsites in good spirits. Each boy was victoriously explaining his own techniques as they walked.

Chapter IV
A Soggy Day

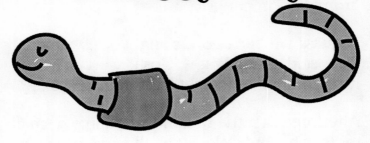

The next day the boys awoke to a day of soft rain and drizzle. Feeling a little distraught because of the weather, John and Dale pulled the sleeping bags over their heads and tried to sleep. The light rain pitter-pattered on their tent ceiling. Sometimes large drops fell from the trees above and sounded like someone had put a water sprinkler on their tent. The frogs were croaking to each other and the robins were singing in the rain.

"This is no good," said John crossly. "I can't sleep with all this racket. Let's get up and get some breakfast. My stomach is starting to grumble. I'm hungry."

"I guess we can't go picking worms tonight," Dale said grumbling. "Gosh, we can't even have a campfire tonight if this rain keeps up."

After breakfast the drizzle turned into a small mist. John and Dale put on their rubber boots and rain coats. Like two grumpy old men, they splashed and stomped over to the Green Hornet. Mark met them at the door. "I think I'll stay inside and read a book for awhile. I don't want to get my wheels muddy."

John and Dale nodded. "What a rotten day," said Dale, as he turned to leave.

Mark asked, "Why don't you come over this afternoon and we can play some table games?"

"Sounds good to me," John said.

Still pouting about the soggy weather, Dale also agreed.

Splashing determinedly through more puddles, the two despondent boys reached Lee's Red Dragon.

"What a bummer of a day," said Dale as he talked to Lee through the screen door. "Do you want to splash around in the mud puddles with us?" he asked.

"No! I'm not going to go out yet," answered Lee. "I want to read up on my butterfly and moth collection books in case I see a new species around camp."

Grudgingly, the boys trudged back to the Blue Nose and played some hand-held video games in their tent. Later in the afternoon they went over to Mark's and played a table game to amuse themselves. By four o'clock that afternoon mist had disappeared and the warm sun peeped out from behind the clouds, giving the boys some hope. Looking longingly at the grey sky John said, "If the rain doesn't come back, maybe we can pick some worms."

We'll just have to wait and see," said Dale.

After supper Lee trudged over to the Blue Nose wearing his rubber boots with his pail, damp cloth, and flashlight in hand. "We can't let a little rain get us down," he said with a contagious smile.

That night Hal and Amharic wandered over to the Blue Nose's campsite. The Waites were sitting around the smoky campfire enjoying an evening drink of iced tea. Susie was playing with her Barbie doll. Lee, John and Dale stood up when Hall and Amharic arrived.

"Hi! My name is Hal and I live up the road beside Amharic's campsite. I think I heard them call my trailer the Golden Eagle," he said smiling as he extended his hand.

Mr. Waite stood up and shook hands with Hal. "Welcome to our humble abode. Please sit down and join us. This is my wife Anna, our daughter Susie, and I am Kevin. The boys told us about their little adventure last night and you certainly have sparked theirs and my interest."

Rubbing his hands together Hal said, "You folks are really going to enjoy the show tonight." Hal laughingly told them about the boy's antics the night before.

The Campfire Boys approached Hal, except for Mark, who was watching from the Green Hornet's outside platform. Mark's parents were sitting by their own campfire.

"You know boys; the rain brings out more worms then on dry hot days. Your pickings tonight should be very good."

Suddenly it was nine thirty and time to start picking worms. The four boys had a personal quest that each one was going to pick the most. Hal showed the boys the best place on the grassy knoll around their campsite to start with.

The stars started to twinkle in the night sky and the moon was just coming up on the eastern horizon. Now was the time. Slowly but surely the worms started to crawl out of their hiding spots one at a time. Each big fat juicy worm lay half their body on top of the damp grass while securing the bottom half in their safe hole. The sun had set about 15 minutes when the boys slowly walked out and began their quest. Picking worms. This time, because they had the knack of sneaking up on the slippery critters, as Hal called them, they were able to catch a few more in a shorter time span than the night before.

"Go over the grass all the way to the other side and then make your way back slowly," called Hal to the boys. "This way the ones you missed will crawl back out again."

Slowly, but surely the boys were gaining momentum as each one took turns picking worms while the other one shone the flashlight. They were getting really excited inside, but kept their movements slow and quiet so they would not send vibrations down to scare the worms away.

Although they still lost some, and only broke a few worms in half, they were successful in picking lots of worms this time.

Hal shared his plans with the Waite's and asked their permission. They thought it would be a good learning experience and approved.

After a half hour, the excited boys walked proudly over to where Hal was sitting and began counting their catch. Between John and Dale they had grabbed 26, and Amharic and Lee had snatched 24. Giving high fives to each other they placed the worms in one pail and handed it to Hal.

"What a great catch you have there. I guess I owe you $2.50 for these fine specimens."

Reaching into his pocket he gave each boy 75 cents. Chuckling, he said, "You all get a tip for the great show that you put on."

Hal crept over to Mark's trailer hanging onto his canes for support. Once there, he raised one cane to wave the other boys over. Mark opened the screen door and listened from his wheelchair, while his inquisitive parents listened from their lawn chairs.

"Now I have one more piece of advice for you," he continued as he looked at John, Dale, and Mark's parents and then at the boys. "Since you're staying here for a few weeks and most weekends during the summer, you can make a profit picking worms and selling them."

Nodding his head while looking at the boys, Hal continued. "Yes, I said selling them. Look around you, there are lots of campers here who go fishing and where do they buy their worms? Downtown, that's where."

The Campfire Boys looked at each other with a grin and gave another high five to each other and Hal.

"Now you have to keep them in a cool place with breathing space or the summer heat will eventually kill them," Hal continued. "You can place them in a Styrofoam cooler underneath your trailer. You only need to dig a hole big enough to fit the cooler with about one to two inches sticking up out of the ground, so a rainstorm doesn't drown them. Inside the cooler you will need to put in grass, leaves and some good earth. Mix it all together and then put in your worms. Next spray a little water on top every few days. That is all the maintenance they will need."

Looking at Mr. Waite he continued, "Get your dad to use a roasting fork to poke a few holes in the lid and place a rock on it to make sure the lid doesn't blow away."

"So, what do you think boys," Hal asked? "Do you want to go into the 'worm selling business'?"

"You bet," said John and Dale together.

"I can't wait to tell my parents," said Amharic.

Mark, looking at his parents, agreed and said, "I want to be the official flashlight attendant."

After the boys returned to their campers, Mark watched solemnly from the Green Hornet's large window facing the grassy knoll. "Tomorrow you can go with them," he thought. "But one of these days I'll move my legs again and then I can get rid of this stupid wheelchair!"

Chapter V
The Plan

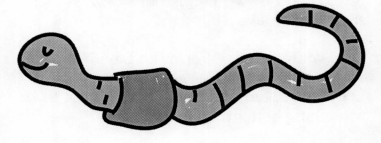

Monday was a day for planning.

The morning weather was cool and partly cloudy. Today the Campfire Boys and their families would be going to their city homes later that evening. They met at Lee's Red Dragon campsite around ten a.m. to discuss their strategy for going into the "Worm Selling Business".

Sitting around the brown picnic table the Campfire Boys set in motion their business plan.

Stretching his two hands out sideways, John said, "Let's make a big sign."

Dale volunteered, "Worms for Sale."

Lee interrupted and said, "No. It's got to be something better than that."

"How about 'Juicy Worms for Sale, inquired John?

Putting his head in his hands, Lee repeated, "No! No! It's got to be a noticeable sign."

"How about in big bold letters 'The Campfire Boys - Worms for Sale'," asked Mark?

"Now that sounds good to me," said Lee looking at everyone and smiling.

"Yeah. That sounds great," said Dale grinning from ear to ear. "With our group name in print, everyone will know who The Campfire Boys are."

Lee announced, "I'll get my mom to make us a few signs. She has really nice hand writing."

"We will have to put the signs up all over," said Amharic. "I can help with that."

Mark eagerly shared, "My dad said he would rake some leaves and mix it with some soil and compost for our project."

John piped up, "Mom said she has an old Styrofoam cooler that we can use. Dad will dig us a hole under our trailer by the shed when we're ready."

The Campfire Boys were really excited and talked about their new challenging adventure for another hour.

Thinking ahead, John said, "We'll only have next weekend to pick as many worms as we can. The Crow Lake Fishing Derby is the following weekend and we have to be ready for that if we are going to make a profit."

"How much should we charge," asked Lee?

"I paid $2.50 a dozen for those skimpy worms I used," said Mark, "and I still caught fish."

Dale proudly suggested, "How about charging $2.00 a dozen, and they bring their own containers?"

Everyone nodded in agreement. Things were looking up for these new business partners.

"My dad said we shouldn't have any problem getting permission from Mr. Schmitt," said John. "He's going to talk to him on our way home this evening."

Dale jumped up excitedly, "I saw a great rock for the top of the worm cooler down by the lily pads over there." He quickly ran down to get it. A few minutes later he came back huffing and puffing. He plopped the rock down by Lee's trailer. "Now this should keep the lid from blowing off."

Amharic said, "I have a nice grassed park across from my house. I'm going to try this new technique of picking worms." Feeling confident, he said, "I'll bring whatever worms I pick with me for next weekend."

"Yes. That is a good idea," said Dale. "We all should try picking as much worms as possible at home this week and bring them for next weekend."

All the Campfire Boys agreed. Finally they all gave high fives and went off to their our campsites.

As Mark propelled himself forward, he said to himself, "Mmmm….Next weekend. It should be a very interesting weekend with my newfound friends. I wonder what new adventures we'll find besides the worm picking business."

Printed in the United States
106771LV00001BB/1-237/A